For Matthew – M.R.

To Orla and Ethan – J.T.

First published in Great Britain in 2023 by Andersen Press Ltd.,
20 Vauxhall Bridge Road, London SW1V 2SA, UK • Vijverlaan 48, 3062 HL Rotterdam, Nederland

1 3 5 7 9 10 8 6 4 2
British Library Cataloguing in Publication Data available. ISBN 978 1 83913 132 5

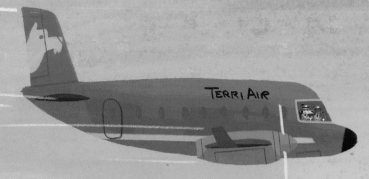

Michelle Robinson   Jez Tuya

TRAINS, BOATS AND PLANES

Andersen Press

Trains and boats
and planes!
Woo-hoo!

Trains and boats and planes!
Land and sea and sky go by on
trains and boats and planes.

All aboard
the steam train.

"Tickets, please.

Let's go!"

Running like a dream, train,
take it nice and slow.
Wheels go click-and-clack, train...

speeding up, *WOO-WOO!*

Running out of track, train?

There's a
tunnel,
phew!

All aboard a big boat, waiting at the quay.

Bon voyage! Set sail, boat. Time to go to sea.

Steady as she goes, boat.

"Rainstorm's on the way..."

Watch the whipping waves, boat!

Safe ashore.
Hooray!

Up above the clouds,
higher than the rain,

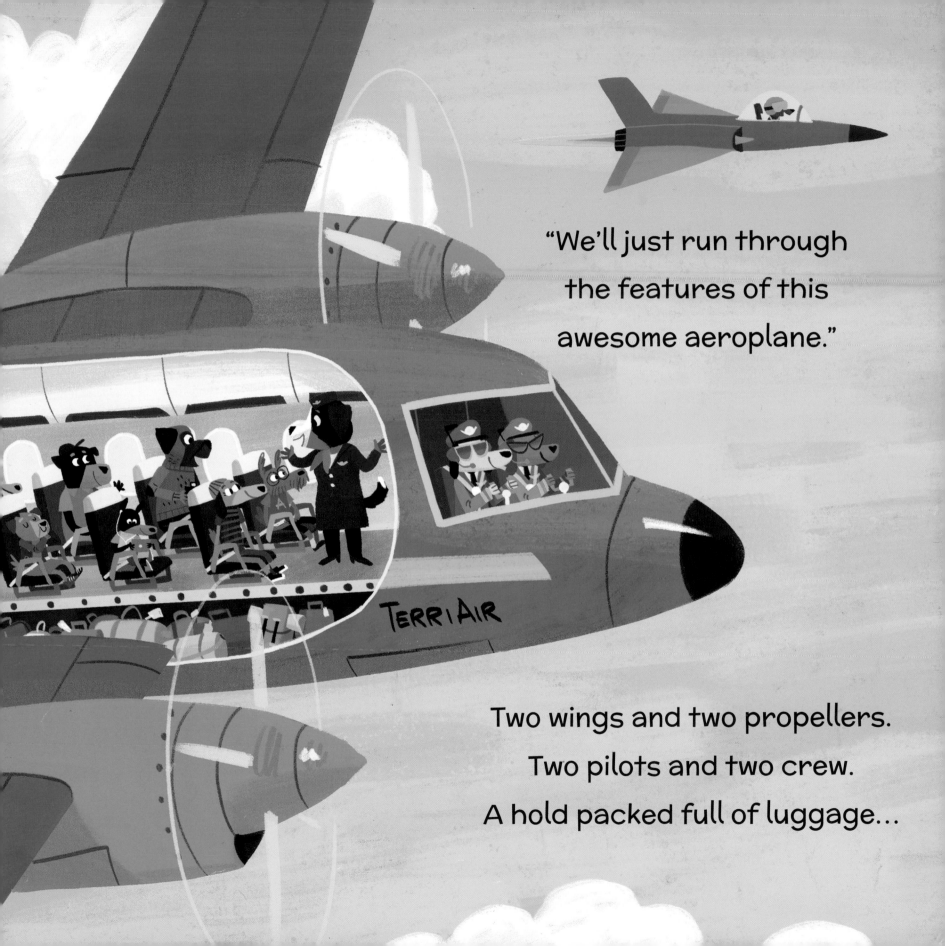

"We'll just run through the features of this awesome aeroplane."

Two wings and two propellers.
Two pilots and two crew.
A hold packed full of luggage...

And the most
amazing view!

Coming in to land, plane.
"Everyone prepare."

Ground crew
standing by, plane.

"Goodbye, folks. Take care."
Everyone piles off the plane.

The journey's almost done.

Board the bus for one last trip...

Enjoy yourselves.
Have fun!

BALLOON FESTIVAL

The passengers are yawning.

What a busy day.

Trains and boats and planes...